How Do Engineers Solve Problems?

Houghton Mifflin Harcourt™

PHOTOGRAPHY CREDITS: COVER (bg) ©Maximilian Stock Ltd./Getty Images; 3 (b) ©Brand X Pictures/Getty Images; 5 (b) ©Darren Kemper/Corbis; 6 (b) ©Jonathan Larsen/Diadem Images/Alamy Images; 7 (t) ©Corbis; 8 (b) ©DariosStudio/Alamy Images; 9 (t) ©auremar/Shutterstock; 10 ©Ryan McVay/PhotoDisc/Getty Images; 11 (b) ©Blend Images/Getty Images; 12 (b) ©Photodisc/Getty Images; 13 (t) ©Alexander Raths/Shutterstock; 15 (t) ©Kristopher Grunert/Corbis; 16 (b) ©Alex Green/Ikon Images/Getty Images; 17 ©Jeremy Sutton-Hibbert/Alamy Images; 18 (b) ©Alan Levenson/Stone/Getty Images; 21 (b) ©Cultura/Igore/Getty Images; 22 (b) ©Rido/Shutterstock

ISBN: 978-0-544-07347-0

15 16 17 18 19 20 1083 20 19 18

4500710588   A B C D E F G

Be an Active Reader!

Look at these words.

engineering

technology

bioengineering

biotechnology

prototype

criteria

Look for answers to these questions.

Why was sunscreen developed?

What makes a sunscreen effective?

How can technology improve our daily lives?

What process do engineers follow?

How do bioengineers help people?

What is a prototype?

What criteria are used?

What are the results of the benefit/risk analysis?

What happens when a prototype fails?

Does the design process change if the prototype changes?

How can I use engineering to solve a problem?

How can I communicate my results?

How do engineers solve problems?

Does technology always improve our everyday lives?

Why was sunscreen developed?

Until the middle of the 20th century, most Americans went outdoors in clothing that covered them from head to toe. Women often used umbrellas called parasols to protect themselves from the sun. As the century advanced, clothing styles changed. People began exposing more of their skin to the sun.

People used to think that sun exposure was healthful. At the beach, they smeared on suntan lotion and sunbathed for hours. But eventually, premature aging of the skin, skin cancers, and other skin problems became health concerns.

Suddenly people looked for ways to protect their skin. Sunscreen was developed to protect people from the sun's harmful ultraviolet rays.

In the late 19th and early 20th centuries, people's clothing covered them and protected their skin from sun damage.

What makes a sunscreen effective?

Sunscreen advertisements show people in bathing suits on the beach. Sunscreen labels in yellow and blue make you think of the sun and sky. But don't choose a sunscreen because you like the ad or the package design. Make sure your sunscreen is labeled Broad Spectrum, which protects you from ultraviolet A radiation (UVA) and ultraviolet B radiation (UVB). Notice the sun protection factor (SPF). An SPF of 30 or higher with Broad Spectrum protection makes sunscreen effective.

The development of sunscreen shows how an engineering process can answer a need and improve our lives.

Which sunscreen would you buy? Why?

SPF 100 SUNSCREEN

Most complete protection available

Stay safe in the sun ALL DAY LONG

ULTRA waterproof and sweatproof

4 FL OZ (118mL)

BROAD SPF 40 SPECTRUM SUNSCREEN

8 FL OZ (237 ML)

Kids SUN BLOCK

Waterproof & Sweatproof

SPF 30 UVA UVB

16 FL OZ (475 mL)

How can technology improve our daily lives?

Many advances have been made in technology since the time women used parasols. Just look around you. Technology is everywhere, from the electric light you switched on to read this book to the zipper in your blue jeans. Technology has changed our daily lives in many ways. People used to listen to music on vinyl record albums, then on cassette tapes, and later on CDs. Today, people can simply download their favorite music from the Internet. Nurses used to check the rate of a patient's heartbeat every few hours by feeling their pulse. Hospitals now use heart monitors to keep track of a patient's heartbeat continuously. Each of these technological changes occurred in response to a need or desire.

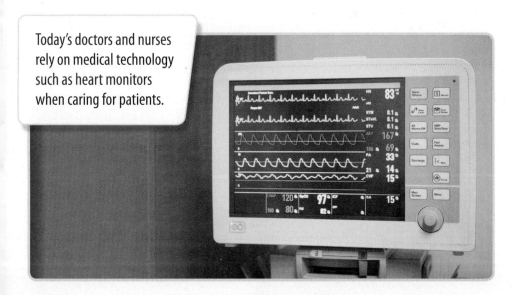

Today's doctors and nurses rely on medical technology such as heart monitors when caring for patients.

What process do engineers follow?

Technological advances are made because of people called engineers. There are several types of engineers. Each type of engineer develops something different. For example, electrical engineers design digital scoreboards for sports events. Civil engineers plan and build roads. Engineers work on finding ways to improve our daily lives. To do this, they follow a logical set of steps called the design process. This process includes five steps.

1. Identify a need, or a problem to be solved.
2. Plan and build a prototype or working model.
3. Test and improve the model.
4. Redesign the model, if needed.
5. Communicate the results.

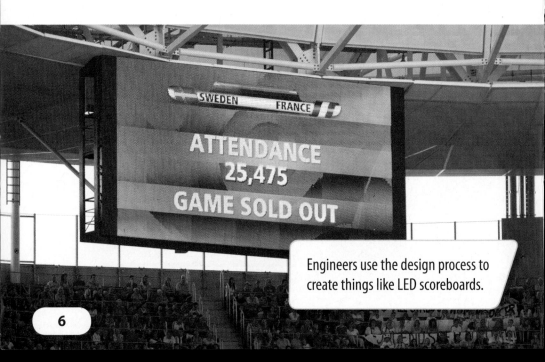

Engineers use the design process to create things like LED scoreboards.

Before refrigerators and freezers were invented, people used icehouses to store ice and keep food fresh.

Defining a problem is the first step in the design process. Asking questions helps to define a problem. For example, the question of how to keep things cold was asked before refrigeration was developed.

As cases of sun-related skin aging and skin cancer increased, someone asked, "How can we better protect our skin from sun damage?" Asking this question helped to define the skin-care problem.

This first step is perhaps the most important step in the design process. After a question is asked, the problem is defined, and engineers decide if it's worth solving. If they agree that it is, they go on to the next step—planning and building the model, or prototype.

How do bioengineers help people?

A bioengineer is a particular kind of engineer who applies the design process to living things: plants, animals, and people. Bioengineering is involved in many medical advances. For example, bioengineers built an artificial heart that can be transplanted into a human body. A type of technology called biotechnology relates to living things, too. The development of sunscreen is just one of the many ways biotechnology has addressed a problem in our daily lives.

Bioengineers had to consider how the human body would react to the chemicals in sunscreen. Sometimes, it is only later that bioengineers learn about an effect of their product. That is why, once a product is developed, engineers keep trying to improve the things they design.

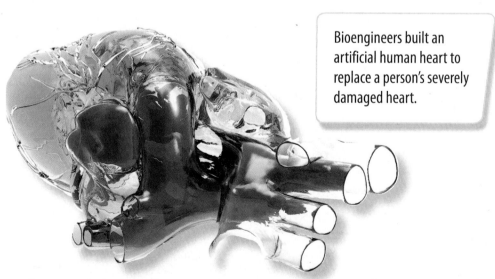

Bioengineers built an artificial human heart to replace a person's severely damaged heart.

An engineer starts the design process by thinking about the problem he or she wants to solve.

Let's imagine a business called Green & Company that produces sunscreen. Mrs. Coleman is a bioengineer leading a project to improve a sunscreen that her company produces. The product does not work as well as it should. Coleman and her team will use the design process to improve it.

First, Coleman and her team identify the problem. People need to be protected from the sun all day. The company's sunscreen needs to be reapplied after two hours. But people often wait too long to reapply it.

Coleman's team completed the first step of the design process. They identified the problem: People don't get all-day sun protection, even when they use sunscreen. Could the team design a sunscreen that lasted all day?

A team will measure and mix the original test model for the improved sunscreen.

What is a prototype?

Next, Mrs. Coleman and her team discuss which ingredients to include in the prototype. A prototype is a test model on which a new product will be based. Coleman and her team talk about what to change about the sunscreen they are currently producing. One bioengineer suggests they add a chemical to make the sunscreen stick to skin even in water. For Green & Company, the second step of the design process, to plan and build, now becomes to measure and mix. The engineers measure and mix up a new sunscreen prototype. The team keeps careful records of the exact amount of each ingredient they use.

Next, the engineers have to calculate how long the new sunscreen protects skin from damage. Mrs. Coleman knows that her own skin will begin to burn in 10 minutes if she isn't protected by sunscreen. She multiplies 10 minutes by the SPF number to learn how many minutes of protection she has in the sun. Sunscreen with an SPF of 15 should last 2.5 hours (10 min × SPF 15 = 150 min = 2.5 hr).

Now, you might think a sunscreen with a higher SPF would protect you longer. But even if you wear SPF 30, you still need to reapply every 2 hours. Sweat and water make sunscreen less effective. After you swim, you might not have any protection at all.

When you're having fun, it's hard to remember when to reapply sunscreen.

What criteria are used?

Mrs. Coleman and her team talk about the criteria they will use to decide if the prototype is a success. The criteria are the standards or values that will be used to measure success. The first standard is time. The main reason for making the prototype is to increase the amount of time sunscreen is effective. The team's goal is at least 8 hours of protection. The second standard is cost. If a product costs too much, people are not going to buy it. Safety is the third important standard for measuring the success of a prototype. If a product isn't safe, a company either redesigns it to make it safe or decides not to produce the product at all. So, Coleman and her team will consider their prototype a success if it meets the criteria of time, cost, and safety.

It's important for an engineer to consider and keep track of the criteria used to measure the success of the prototype.

Like scientists, engineers collect and record data.

Testing and improving the prototype is the third step in the design process. During testing, the team carefully records the amount of time the new sunscreen blocks UV rays. Notice that the steps of the design process are similar to the steps scientists use to conduct an experiment. Engineers, like scientists, develop a hypothesis—a statement that explains a set of facts and can be tested to see if it is supported by data.

Coleman's hypothesis is that the prototype will increase the time of the sunscreen's effectiveness to 8 hours. The team members test and retest the prototype. They collect data. Then, like scientists at the end of an experiment, they study their results and draw a conclusion.

What are the results of the benefit/risk analysis?

The team is happy about the results. Two of the criteria were met. Coleman's team reached its goal of 8-hour sun protection. The second factor, cost, was met, too. The new sunscreen costs about the same to produce as the earlier sunscreen. The third factor, safety, still has to be tested.

The safety of the new product will be decided during the benefit/risk analysis. This is when the engineering team studies the benefits and the risks of the sunscreen prototype. Then they will decide whether to produce the sunscreen or to develop another prototype. What are the benefits of the new sunscreen? Long-lasting protection from the sun and low cost are clear benefits.

Benefit/Risk Analysis for 8-Hour Sunscreen Prototype		
Protection	8-hour protection	benefit
Cost	less than $4.00 per tube	benefit
Safety	?	?

When making a prototype, engineers must consider all the criteria including how safe the product is.

Experts in different fields work together to evaluate the risks and benefits of prototypes.

The next question is "What are the risks of using the new sunscreen?" As far as the team members know, none of the chemicals used in the sunscreen have negative side effects, but they have to be sure. So, Coleman brings a sample of the sunscreen to a dermatologist, a doctor who treats diseases of the skin. Coleman gives the doctor a list of the chemical ingredients used in the prototype. The dermatologist keeps the prototype for a week. He studies the ingredients and Coleman's observations. He determines that one of the chemicals used in the new solution could cause a rash in some people. Another ingredient has recently been identified by medical researchers as a possible cause of skin cancer.

What happens when a prototype fails?

Mrs. Coleman brings the bad news back to her team. There is no way to produce a safe, long-lasting sunscreen with these ingredients. The team discusses redesigning the prototype to make it safer. One bioengineer suggests removing the two possibly-harmful chemicals. Coleman points out that if they remove those particular chemicals, the sunscreen won't last for 8 hours.

Coleman and her team decide that they cannot meet the criteria. Using these ingredients, they can't make a sunscreen that lasts a long time and is safe for consumers. Their prototype has failed the design criteria. They do not complete the last two steps in the design process. They do not redesign the prototype or communicate their results. Sometimes prototypes fail to meet criteria.

A prototype is not always successful.

Engineers often have to create many prototypes before they are satisfied with the result.

You might not realize how often prototypes fail and how many times an engineer tries again. For example, inventor James Dyson was unhappy with his vacuum cleaner. He thought it lost suction strength over time. So, he decided to invent a better vacuum cleaner himself. Dyson thought the more dirt there was in a vacuum cleaner bag, the worse the suction was. Could he make a vacuum cleaner without a bag? Dyson went through the design process. He identified a problem: vacuum cleaners that lost suction. He planned, built, tested, and improved many prototypes. Finally, one prototype met his design criteria. He then communicated the benefits of his product to sell it.

Does the design process change if the prototype changes?

Mrs. Coleman and her team will decide on another approach. Now they will focus on finding a way to inform people when their sunscreen needs to be reapplied. This way, the team's original goal of increasing time for sun protection will still be met. A team member has the idea of having people wear a wristband. A light in the wristband will change from green to red when it is time to reapply the sunscreen. Wristbands are inexpensive and reusable. The sunscreen cost will not increase. The team starts working on a wristband prototype right away. They will go through the same steps in the design process.

Sometimes a new prototype is completely different from the last one tested.

Gather all the ingredients for your prototype.

How can I use engineering to solve a problem?

You can use engineering to solve a problem by following the design process. First, you need to identify a problem. Here's a suggestion. Do you like to drink something when you get home from school? The problem is that so many drinks have too much sugar. You want to drink something bubbly and sweet that's healthful, too.

So, what's the next step? Measure and mix a prototype with these four ingredients for a healthful, delicious drink. First, get out a glass and some ice cubes. Then, get out some club soda, which is carbonated water with no sugar or calories. You also need some 100% fruit juice and some fresh fruit. Orange juice and fresh lemon slices make a good combination. Finally, you need measuring cups.

How can I communicate my results?

Keep careful records of how much ice, water, fruit juice, and fresh fruit you use for your prototype by measuring each ingredient. Start by filling a tall glass with ice. Pour in some club soda and some fruit juice. Top with a slice or two of fresh fruit. Now test your prototype by tasting it. Does it need more club soda? More juice? Use your senses to observe how the drink looks, tastes, and smells. Record your data in a notebook, and then improve on your prototype, if needed. Once you produce a prototype you like, share the recipe with your friends! How did it feel to use the design process to identify a problem, create a prototype, test and improve your prototype, and communicate your results?

Now it's time to taste your prototype!

How do engineers solve problems?

As you have learned, engineers solve problems by following the steps of the design process. But engineering takes more than just following these steps. Engineers look for and discover problems we might not even know exist. They work with other experts to find the best solution to a problem. They use their imaginations to think of creative ways to design prototypes that might solve a problem. They follow guidelines about safety and health. They must accept failure when it happens and have the courage to start over with a new approach. Just think of all the improvements engineers will make while you are growing up!

What do you hope engineers will design next?

Does technology always improve our everyday lives?

The goal of most technology is to help us in our everyday lives. But some technologies may be harmful. One example is a tanning bed. People pay money to lie on a tanning bed. They don't want to protect their skin from the sun-like lights because they want to get a tan.

Engineers created tanning-bed technology because consumers wanted a way to tan in the wintertime. Engineers are now trying to make safer tanning beds. These new tanning beds still might not be completely safe, though. Getting a tan involves exposure to ultraviolet rays, and too much ultraviolet radiation is harmful no matter how a person is exposed to it. Further research and more education are needed so that people will do a better job of protecting their skin from the sun.

Tanning beds are a technology now seen as a health hazard.

Design and Build a Kite

Use the design process to build a kite. Decide on the size and color of your kite. Then gather your materials: colored paper, a wooden dowel, a strip of fabric, tape, scissors, and a spool of string. Cut the paper into a diamond shape. Tape the dowel from one point of the paper diamond to the opposite point. Tape the fabric at one end of the dowel to make the tail. Tie the end of the string to the middle of the dowel. Then test your prototype by flying it. How can you improve your prototype?

Improve a Product

Think of some products you use. Choose one that you think could be improved. Think of the steps of the design process. What is the problem you need to define? What kind of prototype might be made? How would you test the prototype? Write a proposal for improving your product, and present your proposal to the class.

bioengineering [by·oh·en·juh·NIR·ing] The application of the engineering design process to living things.

biotechnology [by·oh·tek·NAHL·uh·jee] The product of technology used to benefit organisms and the environment.

criteria [kry·TEER·ee·uh] The standards for measuring success.

engineering [en·juh·NEER·ing] The use of science and math for practical uses such as the design of structures, machines, and systems.

prototype [PROH·tuh·typ] The original or test model on which a product is based.

technology [tek·NAHL·uh·jee] The use of scientific knowledge to solve practical problems.